A Sack
Full of Feathers

For David, Elizabeth and Noah, with love. —D.W.

*For my dad, Allan Gurbach, who knew the value of hard work
and a practical joke.* —C.R.

Text copyright © 2006 Debby Waldman

Illustrations copyright © 2006 Cindy Revell

Library and Archives Canada Cataloguing in Publication

Waldman, Debby

A sack full of feathers / Debby Waldman; illustrations by Cindy Revell.

ISBN 1-55143-332-x

I. Revell, Cindy, 1961- II. Title.

PS8645.A457S22 2006   jC813'.6   C2006-901679-8

First published in the United States 2006

Library of Congress Control Number: 2006924162

Summary: In this retelling of a Jewish folktale, Yankel does not realize the harm done by the stories he spreads—
at least not until the rabbi teaches him an important (albeit gentle) lesson.

Orca Book Publishers gratefully acknowledges the support for its publishing programs provided by the following agencies:
the government of Canada through the Book Publishing Industry Development Program, the Canada Council for the Arts,
the government of British Columbia, and the British Columbia Arts Council.

Design and typesetting by Lynn O'Rourke.
Interior and cover artwork created using acrylics.
Scanning: Island Graphics, Victoria, British Columbia.

Orca Book Publishers
Box 5626 Stn. B
Victoria, BC Canada
V8R 6S4

Orca Book Publishers
PO Box 468
Custer, WA   USA
98240-0468

Printed and bound in Hong Kong

09 08 07 06 • 5 4 3 2 1

A SACK FULL OF FEATHERS

Story by Debby Waldman
Illustrations by Cindy Revell

ORCA BOOK PUBLISHERS

In the village of Olkinik lived a boy named Yankel, who loved to tell stories. Not his own stories, mind you. Yankel found other people's stories far more interesting. And because his father owned the village store and the store was where everyone gathered to trade news, Yankel was able to overhear many stories, which he took great pride in repeating.

"Oy! Can you believe what I did?" Reb Wulff was laughing so loudly he could barely get the words out of his mouth.

"What? What did you do this time?" The men pressed closer to the baker, eager for more.

"I lost my glasses, again!" Reb Wulff paused and let out such a thunderous whoop that Yankel dropped his broom. "And so I put salt in the rugelach, not sugar! Salt! Like stones those rugelach would have tasted!"

The men erupted in laughter.

"That's nothing!" one called out. "My wife's rugelach taste like candle wax!"

And another piped up, "My wife's taste like old shoes!"

Yankel slipped out the door to tell his friends the latest news.

So he never heard the end of the story, where Reb Wulff told the men how his wife discovered the mistake and made him throw away the dough. "Even the chickens wouldn't eat it!" he said.

At the schoolyard, Yankel was so busy telling his latest story that he didn't see the rabbi standing nearby.

"That crazy Reb Wulff!" Yankel said. "He put salt in the rugelach. Not sugar! Salt! Imagine that! Those rugelach tasted like stones!"

"Yech!" Yankel's friends said to each other. "I'll never eat anything from Reb Wulff's bakery again!"

Returning to the store that afternoon, Yankel hurried past the bakery. He did not notice the customers crowded inside, or the rabbi, standing by the door, biting into rugelach so sweet and tender it all but melted in his mouth.

Back at the store, Yankel was dusting the shelves when he heard a commotion by the fabrics. Turning, he watched, fascinated, as Freya Silinsky tried to grab a bolt of black fabric from Rifke Meisel's hands.

He was out of the shop so quickly that he was long gone by the time Rifke and Freya agreed that perhaps they could share the cloth. They apologized to each other and together carried the fabric to the front of the store.

Meanwhile, at the schoolyard, Yankel's friends gathered around him.

"Freya Silinsky lives next to me," Yossi Bergman said. "She yelled at my dog once, for barking. She's mean!"

"That's what I'm saying," Yankel said. "You've never seen anything like it. They were fighting like cats!"

He waved his hands wildly and made loud shrieking noises. The boys joined in. Soon their commotion could be heard clear across the schoolyard, which is where the rabbi happened to be taking his afternoon stroll.

When Yankel returned to the store, his father greeted him. "Yankele, where have you been?" he asked, handing him a dust rag. "I found this on the counter by the fabrics."

Yankel took the dust rag and wandered to the other side of the store. There, beautiful Tovah Fleischer, the butcher's daughter, lovingly fingered a lace tablecloth. Up behind her came Levi Weinberg, the cobbler's son. Levi slipped his arms around Tovah. She looked over her shoulder and laughed. Levi lifted the tablecloth out of her hands and draped it over her head so she looked like a bride. As he stood, smiling, she walked around him the way a bride would circle her groom at her wedding.

Then Levi pulled Tovah to him and gave her a kiss! And she kissed him back!

Yankel could not believe his eyes. Wasn't Tovah supposed to marry the rabbi's nephew? Hadn't he heard that last week in the store?

Of course he had! And he'd told all of his friends!

Dropping his rag, Yankel hurried toward the door. He had almost reached the schoolyard when he felt a hand on his shoulder.

"Finished with your dusting, Yankel?" the rabbi asked.

"Yes, sir," he said.

The rabbi looked at him sternly.

"No, sir," Yankel said, looking down at his feet.

"Where were you going in such a hurry, then?"

Yankel swallowed.

The rabbi waited.

"I saw Levi Weinberg kissing Tovah Fleischer," Yankel said finally. "I wanted to tell my friends."

"Just as last week you told them that Tovah was marrying my nephew?" the rabbi said.

Yankel was confused. How did the rabbi know what he was telling his friends?

"Stories spread, Yankel," the rabbi said. "You tell your friends, your friends talk to each other, people overhear and the story goes where it goes. My nephew is marrying a lovely girl from another village. How do you think his bride would feel if she heard he was marrying Tovah?"

The rabbi didn't wait for an answer. They had arrived at his house, and he was reaching for a brown sack from a corner near the door.

"I have a job for you," he said, presenting the sack to Yankel.

Yankel peered inside. "This sack is full of feathers."

"Indeed it is," the rabbi said. "And I want you to put one on every doorstep in the village."

"On every doorstep? A feather? But why?"

"You will understand soon enough."

It was late in the afternoon. As Yankel laid a feather on the doorstep of his father's store, he watched the men gathered by the window. He tried to make out what they were saying, but a breeze stirred the feathers in the sack, and he was reminded of his task.

The next stop was Freya Silinsky's house. He hurried through the front gate and dropped the feather, not even bothering to see where it landed. He did the same thing at the houses of Levi Weinberg, Mendel the butcher and Reb Wulff. When he came to Rifke Meisel's house, he saw her through the window, her back to him, and he set down a feather and ran.

On his way back to the rabbi's house, Yankel wondered what story he would tell his schoolmates tomorrow. If only he could stop at the store! He was so wrapped up in his thoughts that he barely felt the gust of wind that sent a cloud of feathers swirling behind him, up toward the sky.

The rabbi was waiting for Yankel. "That's a good boy," he said when Yankel held out the empty sack. "Now I want you to get all the feathers, put them back into the sack and bring them here to me."

"Excuse me, Rabbi?"

"Go and get all the feathers and bring them back. Hurry, Yankel, for soon it will be dark, and the feathers will be hard to find."

"Bring back all the feathers?" Yankel asked.

"Go," the rabbi said, nudging him out the door.

Yankel felt as if someone had tied his stomach in knots. How would he ever find all the feathers before dark? And even if he did, how would he then have time to find a story to tell his friends tomorrow?

"Yankel Liebovich! What are you doing?" Yankel looked up from Freya Silinsky's hedge to see her staring down at him, large and imposing.

"I'm looking for a feather," he explained.

"Are you crazy?" she asked. "For what do you need a feather? Your mother has feathers in the pillows at your house. I have feathers on the chickens in my coop. You want a feather? I'll get you a feather."

"No, no," Yankel said. "Not any feather. A feather I left here earlier today."

"Any feather you left here blew away a long time ago, Yankel Liebovich. Why would you leave a feather on my doorstep anyway?"

"The rabbi told me to," Yankel said.

"Are you telling me a story, Yankel?"

"No, no," Yankel stammered. "I am telling the truth. But if your feather is gone, then I must go too, for I have many feathers to find before the sun sets."

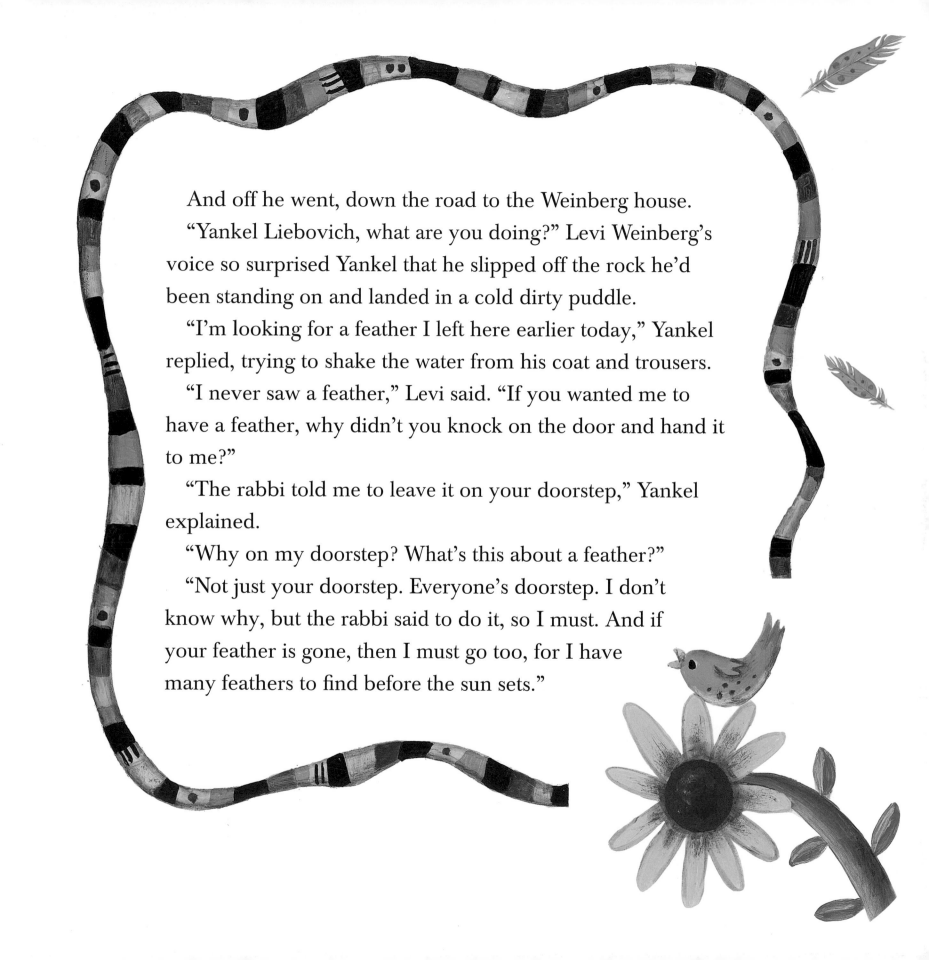

And off he went, down the road to the Weinberg house.

"Yankel Liebovich, what are you doing?" Levi Weinberg's voice so surprised Yankel that he slipped off the rock he'd been standing on and landed in a cold dirty puddle.

"I'm looking for a feather I left here earlier today," Yankel replied, trying to shake the water from his coat and trousers.

"I never saw a feather," Levi said. "If you wanted me to have a feather, why didn't you knock on the door and hand it to me?"

"The rabbi told me to leave it on your doorstep," Yankel explained.

"Why on my doorstep? What's this about a feather?"

"Not just your doorstep. Everyone's doorstep. I don't know why, but the rabbi said to do it, so I must. And if your feather is gone, then I must go too, for I have many feathers to find before the sun sets."

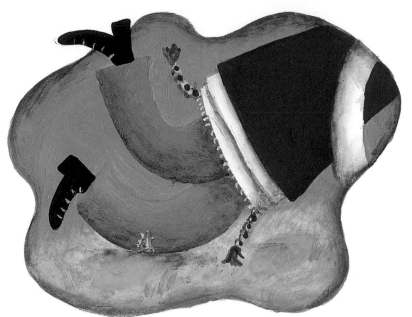

At the home of Mendel the butcher, Tovah's father, Yankel tripped on a loose cobblestone and tore his trousers. He didn't find a feather.

At the home of Reb Wulff, he had to fight off hungry cats who thought he was after their food. He didn't find a feather.

At the home of Rifke Meisel, he thought he found a feather, but when he got closer he saw that it was a dead bird, killed, no doubt, by Reb Wulff's cats.

By the time Yankel returned to the rabbi's house, the sun
had set. A full moon lit the sky. The silvery stars looked almost
like the feathers he'd lost that afternoon. He was tired, hungry,
wet and scratched. And very, very unhappy.

The rabbi, on the other hand, was pleased to see him.
"Yankele! You have returned! Show me what you have!"

Yankel turned the sack upside down and shook it. Nothing
came out. He turned it inside out, just to be certain.

"I found no feathers, Rabbi," he said. "I looked and looked."
He pointed to the tear in his trousers and the mud stains on
his coat in case the rabbi doubted his effort. "They're gone.
I can't get them back."

"And so it is with the stories you spread, Yankele," the rabbi said, motioning Yankel to the table, where a bowl of steaming soup, a thick slice of bread and a plate of rugelach awaited him. "Once you tell a story, you cannot take it back. It goes where it goes, and you cannot say where or how or when. Think of that next time you tell a story, Yankel—and make sure the next story you tell is your own."

Yankel finished his bread and soup. Then he ate all the rugelach, which seemed unusually tender and sweet. He thanked the rabbi for the lesson and went out to the road.

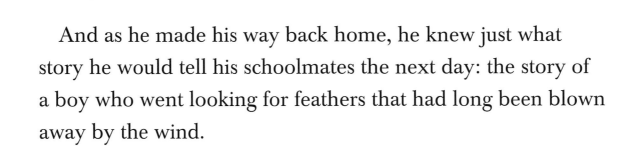

And as he made his way back home, he knew just what story he would tell his schoolmates the next day: the story of a boy who went looking for feathers that had long been blown away by the wind.